Hooray for Our Heroes!

By Sarah Albee
Illustrated by Tom Brannon

Printed in the U.S.A.
ISBN: 1-40371-432-0 (X) 1-40371-493-2 (M)

06 07 08 LBM 10 9 8 7 6 5 4 3
14256 Sesame Street 8x8 Storybook: Hooray for Our Heroes!

Hello there, everybodee! It is I, your furry superhero pal, Super Grover! Today I am going to tell you what the word "hero" means. A hero is someone who you see in comic books and cartoons. Heroes are make-believe.

This hero lived a long time ago, Big Bird. Are there any heroes still around today?
Sure, Elmo! I'll bet we can find some right here in our neighborhood. Let's go look!
GENERAL HELPED·A·TON
HERO

First of all, a hero has a special uniform, similar to the outfit that I am wearing, with a cape on the back and a letter on the chest. I do not see anyone else wearing a hero uniform, do you?

My hero
is my uncle. He's a
police officer. He helps
keep the people in
my neighborhood
safe.

And, of course, everyone knows that heroes have very large muscles and are very strong. No one around *here* is especially strong.

Firefighters are my heroes. They rescue people who are in trouble—and they put the safety of others first.
SSFD

Heroes move with lightning speed. No one around *here* can do that.

I think ambulance workers are heroes. Look how fast they move to help people—all the time!
911
AMBULANCE

Of course, heroes must also be able to fly. Aside from yours truly, no one around *here* can do that.

Uh-excuse me.
Can I get a little
help here?

And heroes must be able to leap tall buildings in a single bound.

Heroes are famous. They are never the people that we see walking around our own neighborhoods.

How would you know a hero if you saw one? That is a very good question! And I, Grover, will answer it for you. For starters, heroes definitely do not wear glasses.

Sure!
Our science teacher is
our hero! She really loves
science and it's fun
learning from her.

And heroes do not just sit around, waiting for things to happen.

The lifeguard is my hero. He makes sure everyone stays safe when they're swimming.

Heroes rescue people who need help. I do not see anyone around here being rescued, do you?

Thanks for coming to the rescue, Doctor. You and your staff are all my heroes!
Congratulations, sir! You've got twins!
Waaaah!
Waaaah!
AUTOMATIC DOOR

Heroes are people you look up to.

My brother is my hero. He plays baseball with me and helps me with my homework. I hope I'll be just like him when I'm bigger.

Heroes save the day!

Good defense today, honey.
Thanks, Mommy. You're not just my coach. You're my hero, too.
You saved the game!

I hope that now you understand what it means to be a hero. Thank you!